DOODLE ART ALLEY BOOKS

JANE AUSTEN COLORING BOOK • VOLUME 17

Samantha Snyder

Copyright © 2019 Doodle Art Alley.
All rights reserved.

Jane Austen Coloring Book is available at special discounts when purchased
in quantities for educational use, fundraising, or sales promotions.
For more information, contact: info@akabooks.com

Cover images © 2019 by Doodle Art Alley.

Cover design by Zaccarine Design, Inc.

ISBN-13: 978-0998832289
ISBN-10: 0998832286

This edition is published by aka Associates.
www.akabooks.com

Doodle Art Alley Books

Emma

A Party is a party.
But a party on a summer's eve, mmm!
Emma
Jane Austen

Better be without sense than misapply it as you do.
Jane Austen - Emma

I Always deserve the best treatment because I never put up with any other
Emma
Jane Austen

Doodle Art Alley ©

Doodle Art Alley ©

Lady Susan

Doodle Art Alley ©

I write only to bid you farewell. The spell is removed; I see you as you are.
Jane Austen
Lady Susan

Where There is
Disposition
to Dislike a
Motive will
Never be wanting.
Jane Austen
Lady Susan

Doodle Art Alley ©

I cannot help thinking that it is more natural to have flowers grow out of the head than fruit
LETTERS
Jane Austen

Jane Austen
I do not want People to be very agreeable, as it saves me the trouble of liking them a great deal.
Letters

Indulge your imagination on every possible flight.
Jane Austen
letter

Which of all my important nothings shall I tell you first?
Letters Jane Austen
Doodle Art Alley ©

Doodle Art Alley ©

Mansfield Park
Doodle Art Alley ©

Mansfield Park
But indeed I would rather have nothing but tea
Jane Austen

Doodle Art Alley ©

Doodle Art Alley ©

Jane Austen
Those who have not
MORE
must be
satisfied
with what they have.
Mansfield Park

We all have our best guides within us, if only we would listen
Mansfield Park
Jane Austen
Doodle Art Alley ©

Northanger
Abbey
Doodle Art Alley ©

Doodle Art Alley ©

It is well to have as many holds upon happiness as possible
Northanger Abbey
Jane Austen
Doodle Art Alley ©

Doodle Art Alley ©

There is nothing I would not do for those who are really my friends. I have no notion of loving people by halves, it is not my nature.
Jane Austen
Northanger Abbey

Doodle Art Alley ©

Persuasion
I am not fond of the idea of my shrubberies being always approachable.
Jane Austen

Doodle Art Alley ©

Persuasion
None of us want to be in calm waters all our lives
Jane Austen

Doodle Art Alley ©

Persuasion
You pierce my soul. I am half agony, half hope... I have loved none but you.
Jane Austen

Pride
and
Prejudice

How much sooner one tires of any thing than of a Book! — When I have a house of my own, I shall be miserable if I have not an excellent library.
~ Pride and Prejudice @ Jane Austen

I have been MEDITATING on the very great pleasure which a pair of FINE EYES in the face of a pretty woman can BESTOW.
Pride and Prejudice
Jane Austen

Doodle Art Alley ©

One can NEVER have too Large a Party
Pride and Prejudice
Jane Austen
Doodle Art Alley ©

Doodle Art Alley ©

Pride and Prejudice
Jane Austen
What are MEN to ROCKS and Mountains?
Doodle Art Alley ©

Doodle Art Alley ©

Doodle Art Alley ©

I am no indiscriminate novel reader.
The mere trash of the common circulating library I hold in the highest contempt.
Jane Austen
Sanditon

Those who tell their own story must be listened to with caution.
Sanditon
Jane Austen

Doodle Art Alley ©

I Abhor every
Common-Place
phraSe
by which Wit is
intended.
Jane austen
Sense and Sensibility

Jane Austen
Sense and Sensibility
I wish as well as everybody else, to be perfectly happy; but I like everybody else, it must be in my own way.

Jane Austen
The whole country about them abounded in good walks
Sense and Sensibility
Doodle Art Alley ©

Doodle Art Alley ©

Doodle Art Alley ©

Doodle Art Alley ©

Jane Austen

December 16, 1775 – July 18, 1817

Jane Austen was an English author. Her novels are considered literary classics, bridging the gap between romance and realism.

Sense and Sensibility, *Pride and Prejudice*, *Mansfield Park*, and *Emma* were published between 1811 and 1815. Her novels *Northanger Abbey* and *Persuasion* were published in 1818, after her death. *Sanditon* is an unfinished novel that Austen initially called *The Brothers* and was later titled *Sanditon* upon its publication in 1925. Jane Austen also wrote numerous letters to her sister and friends describing births, deaths, scandals, and family experiences.

Although not widely known in her own time, Austen's satirical novels of love gained popularity after 1869, and her reputation soared in the 20th century, earning her a place as one of the most widely read writers in English literature. Her books have been adapted numerous times as feature films and television movies and miniseries.

Doodle Art Alley Books

ABOUT DOODLE ART ALLEY

Samantha Snyder is the author of more than 20 award-winning and best-selling coloring books in the Doodle Art Alley Books series including *Attitude Is Everything, Believe in Yourself, Imagination Will Take You Everywhere,* and *Mistakes Are Proof That You Are Trying.*

She has been doodling her whole life. While teaching elementary school, she often drew up coloring pages and printables for her students and fellow teachers. She decided to start sharing her creations and in 2008, Doodle Art Alley was founded.

A quick glance at a doodle may show scribbles, random lines and shapes with no meaning or significance. However, with a little love and direction, these drawings have the potential to compete with some of the best artwork there is!

Doodle Art Alley is dedicated to giving those squiggly lines the proper credit they deserve. Who would have thought that such a small and simple idea could possess so much potential?

There are lots of fun doodle art activities, tips, and information to read through and enjoy. Visit **www.doodle-art-alley.com** for hundreds of exciting doodles.

Doodle Art Alley Books